A mode

Reading a
natural activities and interests of the child. The
next most important aid is a series of books
designed to stimulate and interest him and to
give daily practice at the right level.

Educational experts from five Caribbean countries have co-operated with the author to design
and produce this Ladybird Sunstart Reading
Scheme. Their work has been influenced by (a)
the widely accepted piece of research 'Key
Words to Literacy[1]' adapted here for tropical
countries. This word list has been used to
accelerate learning in the early stages. (b) The
work of Dr. Dennis Craig[2] of the School of
Education, U.W.I., and other specialists who
have carried out research in areas where the
English language is being taught to young
children whose natural speech on entering
school is a patois or dialect varying consider-
ably from standard English.

[1] Key Words to Literacy *by J McNally and W Murray,
published by The Teacher Publishing Co Ltd,
Derbyshire House, Kettering, Northants, England.*

[2] An experiment in teaching English *by Dennis R Craig,
Caribbean Universities Press, also* Torch *(Vol. 22, No. 2),
Journal of the Ministry of Education, Jamaica.*

THE LADYBIRD SUNSTART READING SCHEME consists of six books and three workbooks. These are graded and written with a controlled vocabulary and plentiful repetition. They are fully illustrated.

Book 1 'Lucky dip' (for beginners) is followed by Book 2 'On the beach'. Workbook A is parallel to these and covers the vocabulary of both books. The workbook reinforces the words learned in the readers, teaches handwriting and introduces phonic training.

Book 3 'The kite' and Book 4 'Animals, birds and fish' follow Books 1 and 2, and are supported by Workbook B. This reinforces the vocabulary of Books 3 and 4 and again contains handwriting exercises and phonic training.

Book 5 'I wish' and Book 6 'Guess what?' with Workbook C complete the scheme.

The illustrated handbook (free) for parents and teachers is entitled 'A Guide to the Teaching of Reading'.

For classroom use there are two boxes of large flash cards which cover the first three books.

© LADYBIRD BOOKS LTD MCMLXXV

BOOK 3
The Ladybird SUNSTART Reading Scheme
(a 'Key Words' Reading Scheme)

The kite
and other stories

by W. MURRAY

with illustrations by MARTIN AITCHISON

Ladybird Books Loughborough
in collaboration with Longman Caribbean Ltd

The Kite

You can see children on the beach. Ken and Joy are there.

Some children fly kites. There is a big kite, and there are two little ones.

Joy says, "I like kites."

Ken says, "Yes, I want to fly one."

A boy on the beach knows Ken He has a kite. This boy says to Ken, "You can fly this kite."

"Thank you," says Ken.

---

new words	there There fly kite
	kites

red

Ken makes a kite.

Joy says, "Make a red one. I like red."

"Yes," says Ken. "I want to make it red."

Daddy is there. He looks on. "Have you what you want?" he asks.

"Yes, thank you," says Ken.

Mummy comes in. "Can you fly a kite?" she asks.

"Yes, we can," says Joy.

---

new words   makes   Make   red   ask

dog

Ken and Joy fly the red kite.
A dog is there. It wants the kite.
The dog gets the kite and runs off
with it.

"Look," says Joy. "The dog
has the kite. Run after him."

"Get him," says Ken. "Get the
dog."

He runs and Joy runs.

They run after the dog and
the kite.

new words   dog   gets   Get   runs
                Run   after

string

They run after the dog. Ken gets the kite away from it.

"Go away," says Joy to the dog.

"Go away," says Ken. The dog runs away from the children.

Joy runs with the kite. Ken has the string. "Pull," says Joy. "Pull the string."

Ken pulls the string. The kite flies up and away from him. It goes up into a tree.

---

new words   away   from   string   fli

Ken goes up the tree. He gets the red kite from the tree and comes down.

They fly the kite again. It flies up and Joy lets the string go. As she lets go, the kite flies away. They run after it again.

The kite and string come down in the water.

"Look at that," says Joy. "Can you get it, Ken?"

---

new words   down   again   lets   as

A man there has a raft.
It is a big raft. The man sees
the kite in the water.

"Get on the raft," he says.
They get on and the man
gets on.

The water goes very fast. The
kite goes very fast.

The man makes the raft go
as fast as he can.

He gets the kite for Joy
and Ken. They thank him.

new words   raft   very   fast

Ken flies the kite again.
It goes up so quickly that Ken
lets go.

The kite flies up and away.
Then the children see it go
down. Down it goes into the
sea.

Then Joy says, "We have to
get a boat very quickly."

They run down as fast as
they can. They want a boat
so that they can find the kite.

---

new words   so   quickly   Then   the

At first they do not see a boat.
Then they find a man they know.
He has a very fast boat.
He likes to go fast and so do
the children.

"I like this," says Joy.

"So do I," says Ken.

They all look for the red kite.
They do not see it at first.
Then Ken says, "There it is."

The man gets the kite from
the water.

new words   first do not

Ken has the kite and the string. The boat goes very quickly again.

"Go on," says Ken, "we like to go fast." The man makes the boat go very fast.

Then the boat stops.

"Go on. Do not stop," says Joy.

The man does not know why the boat stops.

"It does not go," he says. "I do not know why."

---

new words   stops   stop   does   why

The man tries to make the boat go. He tries and tries again, but it does not go.

"What can we do?" asks Joy.

The man says, "We have to get help. We want a boat to pull this one, but I can see no other boats."

"We can fly the red kite," says Ken.

"Why?" asks Joy.

"To get help," Ken says.

---

new words   tries but help other

They fly the red kite. They want help, but at first no other boat comes to take them back.

Then they see a big boat. The men on this other boat see the kite. They come to help.

The other boat stops. The men on it make the big boat pull the little one.

The big boat does not go very quickly, but it takes them back.

---

new words   take   takes   them   bac

Carnival

It is Carnival. We all like Carnival. We all like to dress up and dance and sing at Carnival.

Don and Rita want to dress up for the Children's Carnival. Mummy helps them to make what they want. She helps them to dress up.

They can see men and women in the Carnival. Some of them dance and sing. Some look on.

---

new words   Carnival   dress   dance
sing   Don   Rita

The children dress up and go to the Carnival with Mummy and Daddy. They are so happy that they dance and sing. Everyone is very happy.

Then the bands play. Everyone there dances as the bands play. Some of the men and women sing with the bands.

The men in the bands do not stop. They go on and on.

Everyone is happy at the Carnival.

---

new words   Everyone   everyone
              happy   bands

There is a Carnival for men and women and a Carnival for children. Don and Rita want to make something for the Children's Carnival.

At first they do not know what to make.

"It must be something we all like," says Rita.

"It must be something for boys **and** girls," says Mummy.

"It must be something big," says Don.

Daddy says, "It must be something to make everyone happy."

---

new words   something   must   be

shoe

The old woman who lived in the shoe

The children help to make a big shoe. It is a very big shoe. They can all get into it.

It is for the Children's Carnival

One girl dresses up as the old woman who lived in the shoe, but she does not look very old.

All the other children look happy. Some of them make a band and dance and sing.

---

new words   old   who   lived   shoe

The balloons

The children buy balloons.

"What can we do?" asks one of them.

"We can write on the balloons," says one of the others.

"What can we write?" asks one little boy.

"Write your name and address," says a big girl. "Write your name and address on the balloon."

They all write. The big girl helps the little boy to write his name and address on his balloon

---

new words   balloons   balloon   you
name   address

"Is your name and address on your balloon?" asks the man.

"Let go your balloon," he says. "Let go the string. Let the balloons fly up. See how far they go."

The children let go the strings, and the balloons fly up quickly.

The boys and girls look up. They look to see how far the balloons go.

---

new words   how   far

The balloons go a long way.
The children cannot see how far
they go.

One of them comes down in
a school. The children of this
school see the balloon come
down. They read the name and
address on it.

"Send it back," one boy says.
"It has come a long way.
It says on the balloon that
we must send it back. Let me
send it back."

---

new words   long   way   of   school
                     Send   send

This red balloon goes a long way. It comes down on the beach. Some children play there. They are little children who do not go to school.

One little boy finds the balloon. He tries to read what is on it but he cannot. He takes it to his mother who is with him on the beach.

His mother reads from the balloon.

"Can we send it back?" the boy asks.

---

new word   mother

hats

This is a market. There are hats to buy in the market.

A mother with her little girl wants to buy hats. The mother buys two, a big one and a little one. She has the big hat and her little girl has the other one.

A balloon comes down in the market. The woman and her little girl do not see it. Can you see it?

---

new words   market   hats   hat   he

After a time letters come
to the school about the balloons.
The children send back letters of
thanks. The letters take a long
time to write.

They find that one letter is
from an old man who is at sea
on his boat. It has come a very
long way.

The old man writes about the
balloon and about his boat. He
has lived at sea a long time.

new words   time   letters   about

The house in the tree

"Come with me," says Ken to Joy. "I know the way to a house in a tree."

"A house in a tree? Is it far to go?" asks Joy.

"No," says Ken. "It is not a very long way."

Off they go. After some time Ken says, "There you are. Look at that. There is the house in the tree."

"Are there people in it? Can you see?" asks Joy.

---

new words   house   people

animals

birds

"No, there are no people there," says Ken.

They get in the house.

Joy asks, "What is it for?"

Ken says, "People come here to look at animals and birds. Some people like to see animals and birds. They like to see what they do and how they live."

The two children look at the animals and birds, from the house in the tree.

new word   animals

Can you read the words without the pictures ?

1 The boy and girl fly a red kite.

2 The dog runs after the kite.

3 The raft goes quickly on the water.

4 The boat goes very fast on the sea.

5 Ken flies the kite to get help.

6 A big boat pulls them back.

7 They dress up for the Carnival.

8 They dance and sing to the band.

9 The old woman lived in a shoe.

10 Her name and address are
on the letter.

11 The balloon goes up and away.

12 The mother buys a hat at the mark

13 There are some animals and birds.

14 There are people in the house.

no new words

Words new to the series used in this book

Total number of words 74